Activities

1. Look at the illustration on the front cover. Name the letters and ask your child to identify the pictures. Point out the mascot character wearing goggles and a scarf who is shown below. Discuss what the mascot is doing each time it appears.

2. Browse through My Very Own Big Dictionary and talk about the alphabet pages and the alphabet scenes. Discuss what appears on each kind of page.

3. Recite the alphabet or sing the "Alphabet Song." Point out how the alphabet pages in My Very Own Big Dictionary appear in the same order as the letters of the alphabet.

4. Turn to the alphabet page or pages for a specific letter and have your child try to identify each picture. Read the word for each picture. Point out that all of the words on those pages begin with the same letter. Encourage your child to ask what's that? when a picture is difficult to identify by name. Begin a list with the heading "Words We Want to Learn."

5. "Go shopping" for food in the dictionary. Make a list of the foods you find on each alphabet page. Make your own lists of favorite foods for these letters. You can make alphabetical lists of other items, such as animals or toys, as well.

6. Search for action words with your child — words like dig or climb or ice skate. Promote better vocabulary understanding by having your child pantomime the action words pictured on the alphabet pages.

7. Encourage your child to think about and compare several pictures. Ask questions like these: Which objects would fit in your hand?...etc.

8. Turn to an alphabet page and identify the pair of letters at the top of the page. Call attention to the way they appear together. Look through old newspapers or magazines, find and cut out other examples of the letter, and paste the letters to the sheet of paper.

9. Open the dictionary to one of the ten alphabet scenes. Ask your child to point out and identify other elements in the scenes whose names begin with a sound for that letter. There is an index to the scenes on the inside of the back cover.

10. Look at each alphabet scene and have your child tell a story about a character or the action in the scene.

Above are a number of exciting activities for children to enjoy with this unique dictionary. You can of course adapt these activities to meet the needs of an individual child.

These exercises and activities should lead to many pleasurable hours with *My Very Own Big Dictionary*. Use these suggested activities to come up with exciting ideas of your own!

By the Editors of the American Heritage Dictionaries
Illustrated by Pamela Cote

Houghton Mifflin Company
Boston • New York

For information about this and other Houghton Mifflin trade and reference books and multimedia products, visit The Bookstore at Houghton Mifflin on the World Wide Web at http://www.hmco.com/trade/.

Manufactured in the United States of America

Library of Congress Cataloging in-Publication Data
My very own big dictionary/ by the editors of the American Heritage dictionaries ; illustrated by Pamela Cote.
p. cm.
Includes index.
Summary: Contains everyday words in alphabetical order with illustrations, activity-filled scenes, suggestions for additional language activities, and an index for the alphabet scenes.
ISBN 0-395-76320-7 (hardcover)
1. English language—Dictionaries, Juvenile (1. Picture dictionaries, English. 2. Picture dictionaries.) I. Cote, Pamela, ill.
PE1628.5.M93 1996
423'.1—dc20 95-43294
CIP
AC

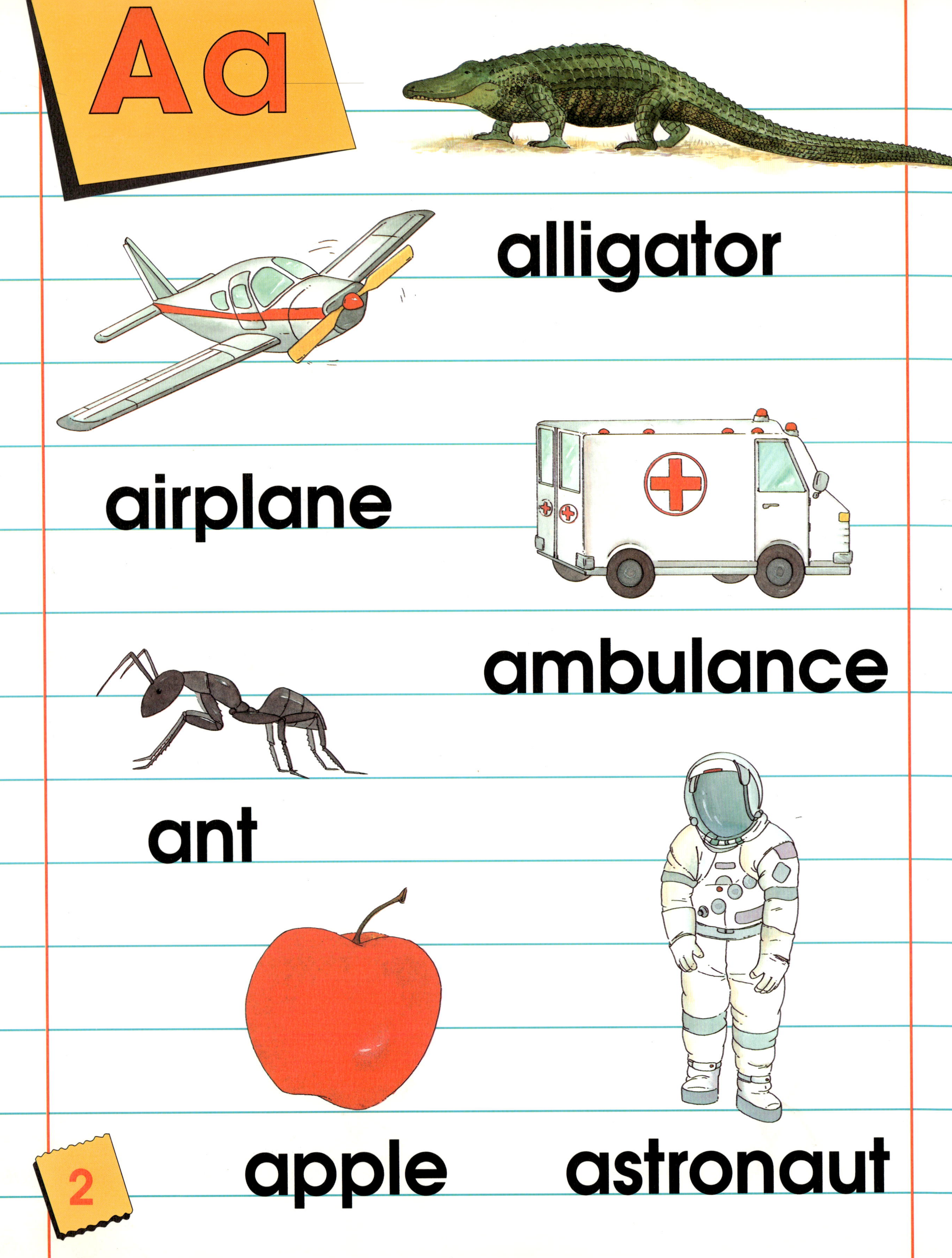
Aa
alligator
airplane
ambulance
ant
apple
astronaut

ABCDEFGHIJKLMNOPQRSTUVWXYZ
ENTRANCE
A
Airport
TO: ALABAMA
TO: ALASKA
TO: AUSTRALIA
A
AIRPORT
TO: ARIZONA

Bb
baby
baker
ball
ballerina
balloon
ballet dancer

banana

band

barn

basket

bear

bell

bird

book

boy

break

bus

butterfly

BEN'S ROOM
BEN

calendar

cactus

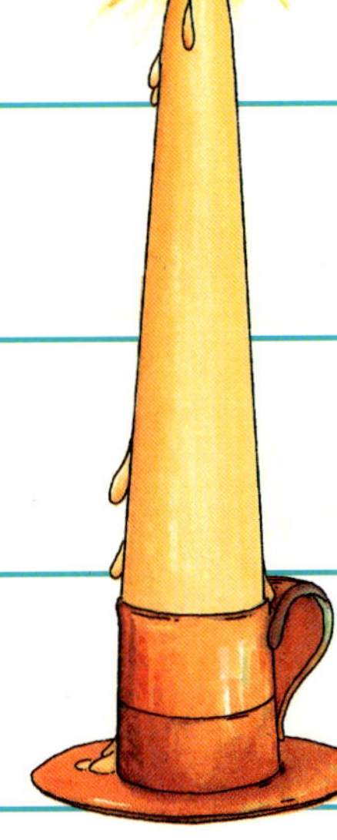

candle

camel

car

carrot

castle

cat

chair

climb

clock

cold

color

computer

cook

cow

cry

CIRCUS
BALLOONS
CHEESE BURGERS
CHEF'S CORNER
COTTON CANDY
CHOCOLATE CANDY
COLD COLAS
THE BIG CHEESE
CAB
CLUCK CLUCK CLUCK CLUCK CLUCK CLUCK
CIRCUS
C
CRACKERS

Dd
dinosaur
dig
dolphin
dog
dragon
draw

DEPARTMENT STORE
DRESSES
SALE
DRAPE SALE
DESSERT DISHES ONE DOLLAR
DELI
DOWN STAIRS
DISC
DIAPERS
DONUTS
DAIRY
DATES
DOG HOUSE SALE
DAISIES DAFFODILS FIVE DOLLARS
D
13

Ee
earth
eagle
egg
eat
elephant

Ff

farmer

firefighter

fish

flower

football

frog

Gg
garden
giraffe
girl
goldfish
goose
grasshopper

Hh
helicopter
hop
horse
hot
house
hug

Ii
ice skate
ice cream
igloo
Jj
jacket
juggle
jump

Kk
kangaroo
kick
king
kite
knock
koala

Ll
ladybug
laugh
lighthouse
lion
lizard
lobster

LUNCH
L
LIBRARY
TO LIBRARY

Mm

MELONS
M
MILK
MOUSE MAGAZINE

Nn

net

nest

newspaper

nickel

night

number

Oo
octopus
onion
open
orange
ostrich
owl

Pp
parade
panda
penguin
parrot
pie
pig

U.S.
POST OFFICE
PARADE
PAINT
POTATO CHIPS
POP CORN
PEANUT BUTTER

porcupine

pour

pretzel

pull

pumpkin

push

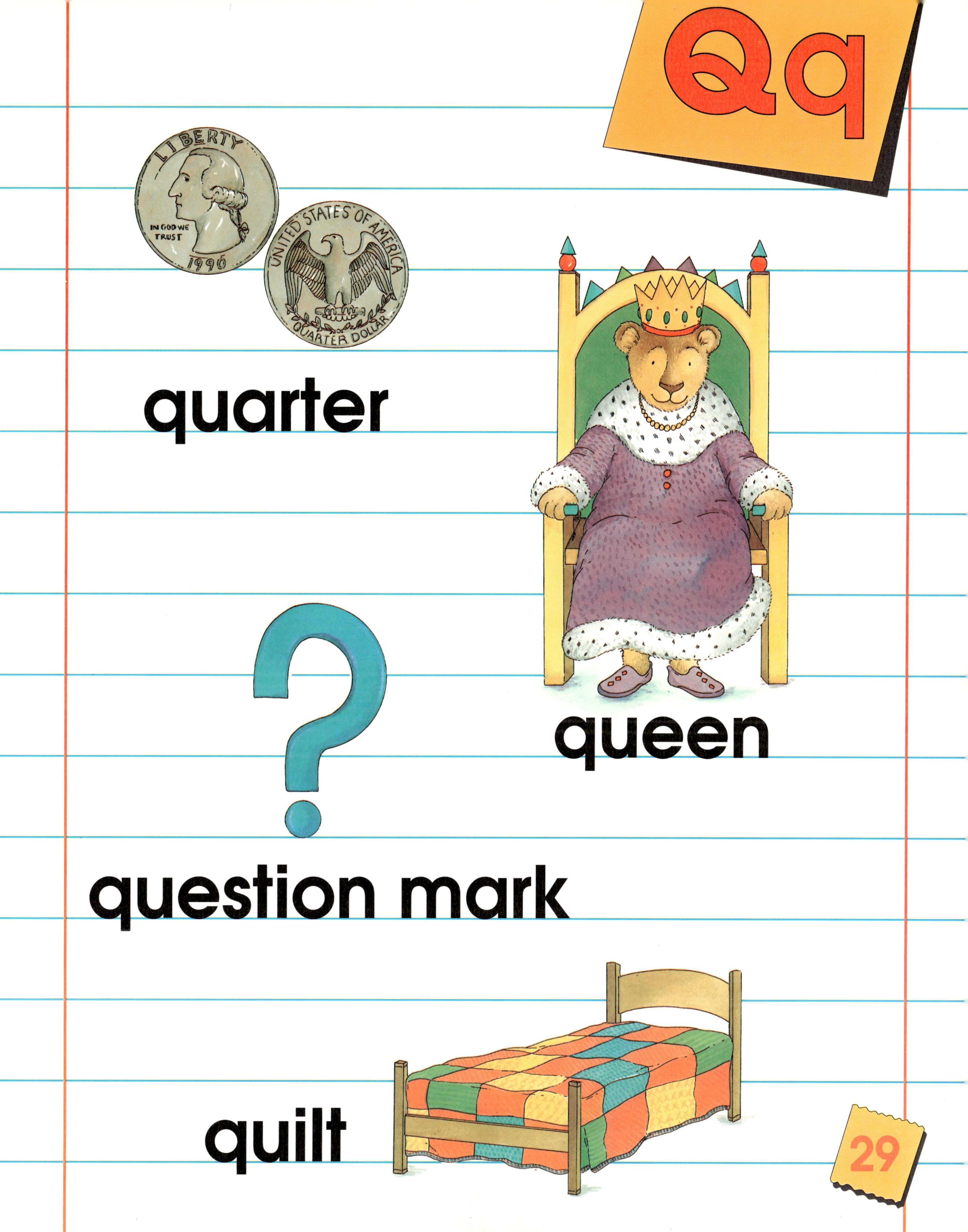
Qq
LIBERTY
IN GOD WE TRUST
1990
UNITED STATES OF AMERICA
QUARTER DOLLAR
quarter
queen
question mark
quilt

Rr

read

rabbit

rhinoceros

robot

rooster

run

RESTAURANT
RANCH
MENU:
ROAST
RICE
RADISHES
RELISH
RODEO
TODAY

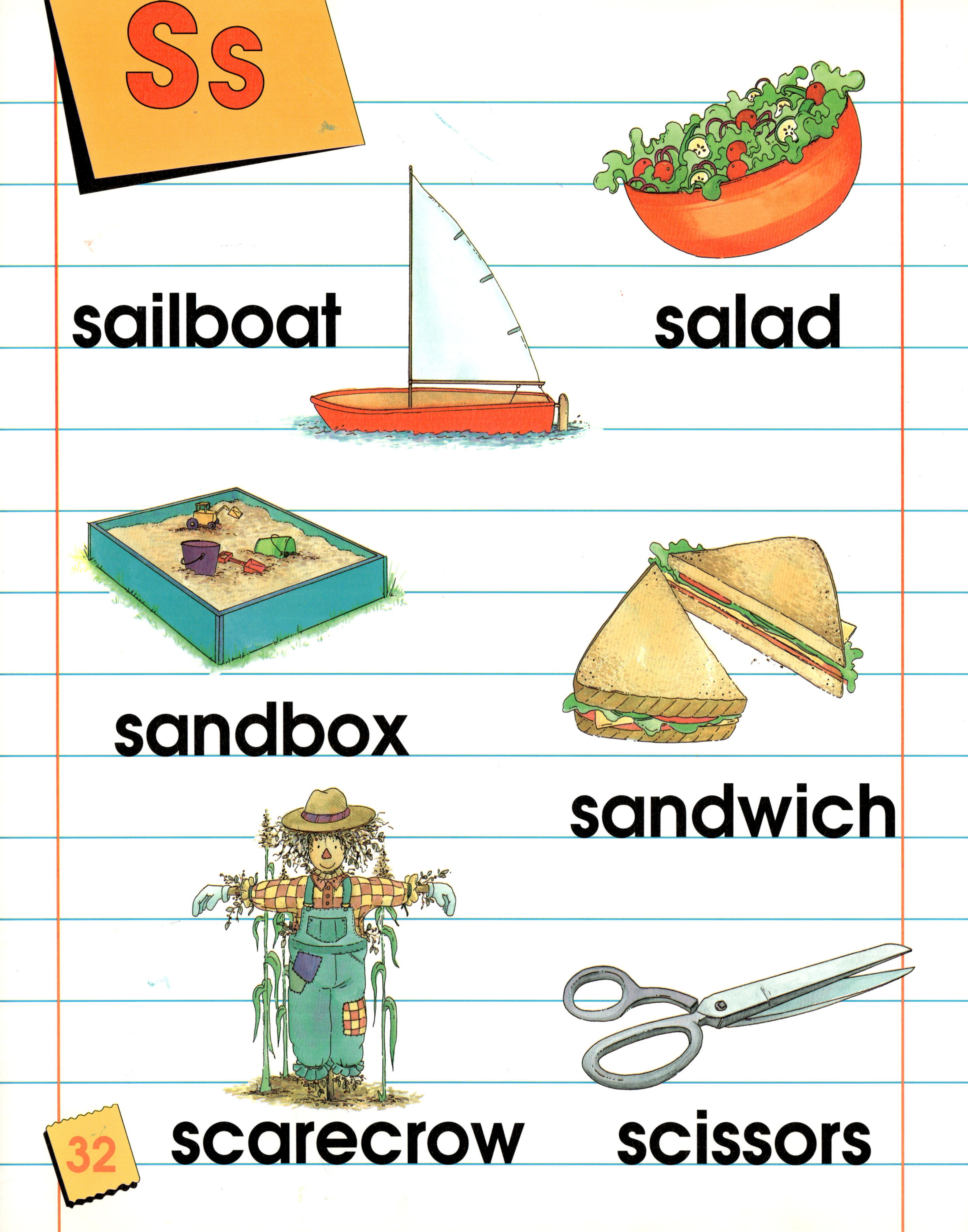

Ss
sailboat
salad
sandbox
sandwich
scarecrow
scissors

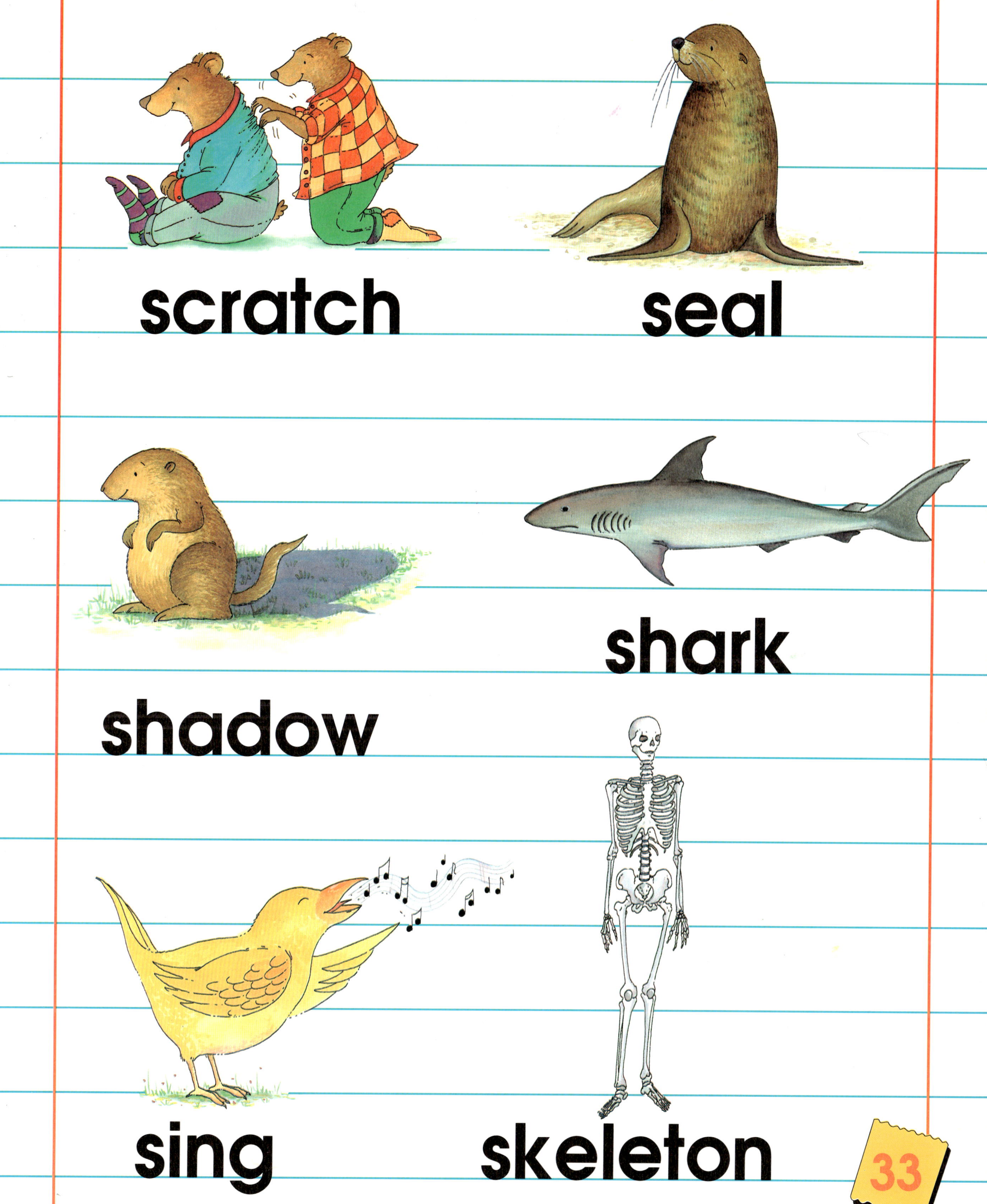

scratch

seal

shadow

shark

sing

skeleton

sleep

snow

soccer

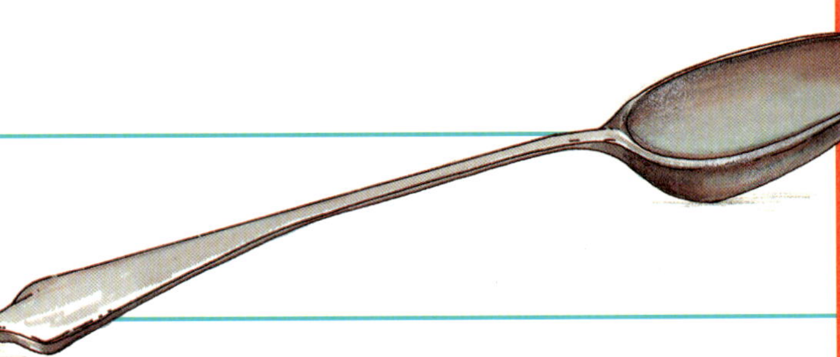

spoon

sun

swim

SEA FOOD
SALE
WHYEVERNOT
17
SALE
SUPERMA
W. MAIN STREET
SCHOOL
STOP
STATUE
7
S
SOUP
SCIENCE
SPELLING
STORIES

Tt
telescope
talk
throw
tie
tiger
tornado
36

TED'S TREE HO
SOCCER TEAM
TEDDY BEAR'S TEA PARTY 10:00
TOAD'S
TEDDY
TODAY TEDDY BEAR'S TEA PARTY
FAIRY TALES

Uu
unicorn
umbrella
uniform
Vv
van
violin
volcano

Ww

wash

wet

whale

wheelchair

woman

write

Xx
x-ray
xylophone
yard
Yy
yo-yo
Zz
ZOO
zebra
zoo
BCDEFGHIJ — HOR — 99876